Ancient Voices

written by
KATE HOVEY

with illustrations by
MURRAY KIMBER

Margaret K. McElderry Books
New York London Toronto Sydney Singapore

To Ivy, Glen, and Ellie Rose
With thanks to Lee Bennett Hopkins for his generous encouragement
and support, Brenda Bowen for making impossible dreams come true,
and Emma Dryden for her kind and skillful guidance
—K. H.

To Kari for steering me through dark passages,
and to Isabella for being the light at the end
Thanks to Kate Hovey, Ann Bobco, and Abelardo Martínez
for their immense patience
—M. K.

Margaret K. McElderry Books
An imprint of Simon & Schuster
Children's Publishing Division
1230 Avenue of the Americas
New York, New York 10020
Text copyright © 2004 by Kate Hovey Gullickson
Illustrations copyright © 2004 by Murray Kimber
All rights reserved, including the right of reproduction
in whole or in part in any form.
Book design by Abelardo Martínez
The text of this book is set in Baskerville.
The drawings for "The Underworld" are charcoal,
conte, and acrylic on hand-stained paper.
The rest of the illustrations are rendered
in oil over acrylic on canvas.
Manufactured in China
2 4 6 8 10 9 7 5 3 1
Library of Congress Cataloging-in-Publication Data
Hovey, Kate.
Ancient voices / Kate Hovey ; illustrations by
Murray Kimber.– 1st ed.
p. cm.
Summary: Twenty-three poems give voice to a variety of
goddesses, gods, and mortals from Greek and Roman
mythology.
ISBN 0-689-83342-3
1. Mythology, Classical–Juvenile poetry. 2. Children's
poetry, American. [1. Mythology, Greek–Poetry. 2.
Mythology, Roman–Poetry. 3. American poetry.]
I. Kimber, Murray, 1964– ill. II. Title.
PS3558.O8749 A82 2002
811'.54–dc21
00-028359

MOUNT OLYMPUS

In the beginning, the immortals
who have their homes on Olympus created
the golden generation of mortal people.

—Hesiod, *Works and Days,* 8th century B.C.

The Cupbearer

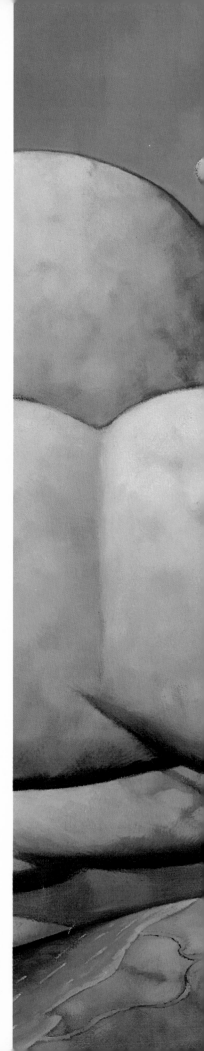

I, Ganymede,
    hail from fabled Troy.
        The king's own son,
        I used to run
free as any shepherd boy
until a giant eagle,
        swooping through the sky,
          dove straight down
          without a sound;
sharp talons gripped my thigh.

Torn from Trojan soil,
    I was hauled far out to sea.
        A frightened hare
        in a deadly snare,
I dangled helplessly.
We crossed a distant shoreline,
    crested mountains, circled round,
        then plummeted like stone.
        Awakening, alone,
I stood, unharmed, on sacred ground.

Now I serve great gods
    on high Olympian thrones
        nectar–fine,
        honeyed wine–
in goblets set with stones.
I'm told I cannot die
    as other mortals do.
        It's troubling, though,
        to never grow;
I hope it isn't true.

I've lost my home, my family,
    so many pleasures, yet–
        it's amazing here!
        This atmosphere
helps me forget,
hollowing each memory
    into an empty shell.
        Can time erase
        a mother's face?
Apparently, quite well.

Like a tapestry lying
    beneath the brilliant sun,
        weathered, frayed
        details fade;
her features come undone.
Still, a precious remnant,
    one small, soft piece I keep:
        I hear her speak,
        feel her breath on my cheek,
each night when I fall asleep.

Ganymede's Complaint

In the great Council Hall
on his gleaming, marble throne
(Nubian gold overlays
the black Egyptian stone)

mighty Zeus sits, waving
an empty amethyst cup.
For the hundredth time this afternoon
I must fill it up.

My legs ache from climbing
this rainbow-colored stair.
Master's in an ugly mood,
demanding special care.

I'll keep the nectar flowing,
making sure I serve him first.
Will nothing ever satisfy
his colossal thirst?

Hera's Lament

Look at him sitting there,
mouth opened wide,
thunderbolts rattling
by his side.
See how he's baring his teeth
like a mule—
why did I marry this
braying fool?
Why? I refused him for
three hundred years!
What made me set aside
my worst fears?
Was it for love, or this
ivory throne?
Would I be better off
all alone?
None of it matters now.
This is my life.
I chose my destiny:
Zeus's wife,
Queen of the Sky—
nowhere higher to climb.
Trapped at the top
till the
end of time.

Ganymede in Hephaestus's Workshop

He taught me how to make a mold,
to pour the molten metal.
He showed me how to operate
the giant forge's pedal—

it makes the bellows swell with air
and stokes the blacksmith's fire.
He taught me how to hammer iron,
to twist a golden wire.

Once, I was allowed to sit
on his amazing throne
made from every possible kind
of metal and precious stone.

Each golden arm moves up and down;
its great, bronze seat can spin.
The whole thing rolls wherever he wants,
both out-of-doors and in.

He built it in his workshop,
the other thrones as well.
He built the gods' great Council Hall,
the palaces where they dwell,

their furniture, fine jewelry,
drinking cups, and bowls.
He even made the thunderbolts
Zeus alone controls.

Today, he finished twenty lamps—
enormous, shining faces
set with brilliant jewel-eyes
on rolling tripod bases!

I watched him leave his anvil,
shifting painfully
the shattered leg beneath him,
braced from heel to knee.

He wiped his neck, his dripping brow,
heaved his shaggy breast.
As I helped him pack his gear inside
a silver-studded chest

I brushed against the leg-iron,
trying not to stare,
but he didn't even notice.
Didn't seem to care.

Hephaestus's Fall

Give me iron, fire, air to feed it,
water for quenching white-hot metal,

my sturdy anvil, tongs, hammer;
I'm a simple blacksmith, not a poet.

But you, mortal, forgetting the story,
stare at my leg and wonder what happened.

I'll tell you. My high and mighty parents,
bound by their bitterness, married to pain,

quarreled with each other for sport or pleasure
day after day. It's still the same.

Zeus's words, like bolts of thunder,
stoked the fire in Hera's eyes.

She hurled them back, and her aim was deadly!
That's when it happened; she hit the mark.

Wounded, he raised his fist above her.
I leaped in front to take the blow

and shot like a comet through the vault of heaven.
Tumbling, senseless, a darkened star,

I fell, they say, from sunrise to sunset;
Helios, driving his chariot heavenward,

watched as the crushing force of Earth
stamped the breath from my broken body.

Kindly Thetis, Ocean's grandchild,
tended me in her briny cave.

But I'm a god; I need no healing.
I can mend whatever's broken,

brace my leg with gold and silver,
bind my heart with an iron band.

I'm a god, no simple blacksmith!
I can mend whatever's broken

with fire, air, water, metal,
my sturdy anvil, tongs, and hammer.

Muses' Song I

Let us go now, veiled in a mist, on swift, sure
feet and climb once more to the starry heavens,
softly, sisters, singing an ageless anthem,
      our voices united.

Nine of us, all daughters of Zeus and Memory,
lived as one mind from the beginning, our hearts
set on song. Our bodies, like fountains, flow on,
      ceaselessly dancing;

from them, all may drink and be filled to brimming.
Songs and great hymns pour from the lips then, fresh tales
spilling out like nectar in honeyed streams—words
      fit for immortals.

This is our gift. Take it and live
      forever.

Muses' Song II
Chant for Athena

Proud,
wise
Pallas Athene,
Gray-Eyed Maiden,
Warrior Queen,
armor-clad and battle-bred,
sprang full-grown from Zeus's head
as suddenly as a thought.
She is
the bold idea
brought
to life,
the goal achieved,
divinely crafted
and conceived.
Sharp her spear,
the aim precise,
arcing over paradise
far and high,
alone,
unseen,
proud,
wise
Pallas Athene.

Athena Speaks of Ares

Olympians despise
his chiseled features,
stony eyes,
the way his chest swells when he stands,
his bloodied hands.

Olympians revile
his frozen heart
and crooked smile.
In his laughter echo sounds
of distant battlegrounds.

THE SEA

Poseidon . . . clad himself in gold
and grasped a well-wrought golden whip,
and mounted his chariot and set out across the waves.
The creatures of the sea arose on all sides
from the depths and gamboled near him,
nor did they fail to know their lord.

—Homer, *The Iliad,* 8th century B.C.

Ganymede's Encounter with Poseidon

Down the rainbow steps from Zeus,
Poseidon, his brother, broods,
slouched in a sea green marble throne
inscribed with multitudes
    of creatures carved to leap and twirl
    on waves of lapis and mother-of-pearl.

No nectar flows between his lips,
no taste of sacred food;
behind his eyes a tempest brews,
the result of an ancient feud.
    Two brothers locked in enmity
    over rulership of sky and sea

glare across the Council Hall,
eyes like flaring embers,
unaware of the Muses' song
or the feasting of other members.
    Poseidon hurls his goblet, stands,
    knocking the pitcher from my hands.

I watch him drive his chariot
down where the dolphins race;
his foam white horses disappear
in the ocean's furrowed face,
    beneath the swirling realm he rules.
    There, the sea god's anger cools.

Aphrodite Talks About the *Venus de Milo* Behind Her Back

Rising from the sea full-grown,
I was made of salt-foam,
    pink shell,
        crushed pearl.
I shine more brightly than the marble girl
carved in my image so long ago.
How many years? I don't know.
Time has little meaning for me;
a goddess, after all, has eternity
to wander in.
She looks so pale, that mannequin!
White is fine for a lifeless thing—
my cheeks are rosy, warm as spring.
Russet and gold adorn my head,
colors plucked from the sea king's bed.
Just look into my eyes!
Every shade of sea and sky's
reflected there.
Amber, coral, the jewels I wear;
agate and every blue-green stone
decorate my copper throne,
yet I'm ignored. It's a disgrace!
You mortals adore that stony face,
dismissing me as nothing more
than ancient myth, forgotten lore.
She is beautiful, but cold:
    Chipped, stained,
      broken,
        old,
while I still have my youthful charms—
not to mention, both my arms.

A Sailor Speaks of Dionysus

He appeared as our ship rounded the rugged cape
dressed in colors of the vine and clustering grape—
a boy, standing alone on the jutting rock,
his robe spread on the wind like a wheeling hawk.
My crewmates—a band of pirates, devils all—
forced me to come about and prepare to haul
ashore where our quarry waited, steeped in dreams,
oblivious to my comrades' evil schemes.

The youth, his eyes half-smiling, drowsed
while the men who seized him, their greed aroused
by thoughts of easy ransom, raced to sea.
I begged them not to harm him, to set him free.
But they bent to the oars, laughing, unaware
of the strong smell of wine that clung to the air,
the growing stillness or the great, green trail
of grapevines climbing up our mast and sail,

spreading swiftly from oar to oar.
Our ship stood still as if it rested ashore.
We struggled with the oars; our rudder froze.
The crew fell silent when the sounds arose—
a chorus of wild beasts—mournful howls—
loud trumpeting—deep-throated growls.
A great bird screeched, and a lion roared.
In terror, twenty men leaped overboard.

The boy, wreathed in a bright green crown,
waved an ivy wand where the men went down,
smiling and pointing toward the pitiful crew,
no longer human, their flesh gray blue,
arms turned to flippers, mouths grown wide.
On strong, curving tails they leaped beside
the ship, sleek bodies lashing and swaying,
each with a fountain of sea mist spraying

from a small spouting nostril atop his head.
I stumbled toward the helm, recoiling in dread
at the prospect of meeting the same dark fate—
a thought too terrible to contemplate.
"Fear not," I heard the strange youth say.
"Set sail for Naxos—don't delay!"
So I, Acetes, brought the ship about,
hauled straight for Naxos and led him out.

Sirens' Song I
Poseidon's Trident

Out of the bottomless deep below
it surfaces like a memory.
An ancient sign all seamen know

heralds the coming of terrible woe.
Towering like a mighty tree,
out of the bottomless deep below,

branches of glistening iron grow
to pierce the sky and stir the sea,
an ancient sign all seamen know

rises ahead of the crash and blow,
striking the ocean suddenly
out of the bottomless deep below;

terror grips like an undertow
the hearts of hapless souls who see
an ancient sign all seamen know,

raised by Poseidon long ago,
surfacing like a memory
out of the bottomless deep below—
an ancient sign all seamen know.

THE UNDERWORLD

For Hades' house is dark, and black
The downward road, the hateful way,
Unwilling and with no way back,
Downward ever, and there to stay.

—Anakreon, fragment from Greek papyrus, 6th century B.C.

The Invitation

I filled his cup, but Hermes shook his head.
"The hour is late. It's time for my routine—
each night, you know, I take the newly dead

to Hades and Persephone, his queen.
You've finished here, so why not come along?
I'll show you things no living soul has seen

and even let you lead the gloomy throng
beyond the private kingdom's iron gates.
Security is tight; those bars are strong.

Admission is determined by the Fates,
who spin and weave a life, then cut the threads
and cast the remnant down to Hades' place.

Old Cerberus won't tear you into shreds
because"—he winked—"we'll keep him occupied;
just toss some food to each of his three heads.

I swear I'll keep you safely by my side!
You'll need a coin for Charon at the landing;
no one goes for free, though some have tried.

That heartless ghoul would leave his mother standing
beside the River Styx without a ride!
Once across, our group will be disbanding;

the dead are judged and shown where they'll abide.
We'll watch the snake-haired Furies lash and goad
each soul until all debts are satisfied.

Now, that concludes an evening's episode
of Hermes' Misadventures with the Dead.
How say you, Ganymede—is it the road?"
I turned him down and headed off to bed.

Sirens' Song II
Persephone's Abduction

We were nymphs, playing in the meadow
on a day like any other,
picking flowers for a simple garland
she was making for her mother.

Then the earth shook beneath us,
roared and opened wide.
On our knees, we heard her screaming
across the sharp divide.

We stretched our arms to reach her,
but the chasm grew too great.
A grinding sound arose from it,
then the crash of a heavy gate.

Thundering out of the darkness
came death-dealing forces;
a dark king in his chariot,
drawn by flint black horses,

rushed past with such fury,
we covered our streaming eyes.
With a mighty groan, the meadow closed
over her echoing cries.

We searched the whole Nysaean plain,
grew wings to comb the sea,
calling, calling to passing ships
for lost Persephone.

The Pomegranate
I. Hades Speaks

Once, you were fresh as the violets
you walked among; fragrant, golden–
an armful of yellow lilies
I plucked from the Vale of Enna.
Now, in my House of Shades,
    the blossom fades.

On your cheek, a rose turns to ashes;
bright ringlets to plaited straw.
Frail as the poppies of Morpheus,
Lady, your proud head bows.
No comfort, no sleep;
    you constantly weep.

Go, Persephone,
before my heart changes.
But take this, Aphrodite's emblem,
my parting token of devotion,
each seed, meadow-sweet.
    Taste one.   Eat.

The Pomegranate
II. Persephone Speaks

Mother, they cast a blood-red glow,
heaped in the hollow of his hand,
bright as embers—like precious beads
saved from a broken strand.

So cool to the touch, sweet to my tongue—
how could I eat just one?
Why, for the sake of seven seeds,
must I leave the sun

to sink beneath the earth again,
down where Hades waits
by the foul mouth of the River Styx
beyond those terrible gates?

Mother, tell me it isn't true.
I'm to become his wife?
How could you send me back to him—
you, who gave me life?

The Pomegranate
III. Demeter Speaks

What good is this land to me?
What is all the wide earth
if you are lost?
For you, child, did I forsake Olympus,
the gods' golden company,
my high throne.
For swallowing you—my only seed—
innocent earth has reaped
an unholy harvest.
Look at it—leafless,
scorched by my bitterness,
but faithful, still,
to the one who did the wounding.
Even now, sweet smoke rises
from a meager sacrifice, reminding me;
to these earthborn tribes
    I am also Mother.

Spring Round
(Nymphs' Song)

Deep in the earth a light
shines through winter's night;
    Persephone lies weeping.

Up from frozen ground
echoes a murmuring sound,
    Persephone's sweet singing.

Tapestries of green
spread out to greet our queen—
    Persephone's arising!

THE FOREST

But look! Diana with her troop of girls
Came winding round the sides of Mt. Maenalus,
Showing the prizes of the chase.

—Ovid, *Metamorphoses,* 1st century A.D.

Muses' Song III
Composed by Apollo
to Honor His Twin

Everywhere Diana goes, we follow,
bearing baskets woven of green willow
filled with every healing herb and flower
gathered from Diana's sacred bower.

Maidens of the village, mountain dryads,
forest nymphs, and river-dwelling naiads
chatter all around her like young sparrows
when Diana shoots her golden arrows.

Far ahead, a wounded stag is swaying;
seven Spartan hounds surround it, baying.
Shouts and cheers announce the chase's ending,
while Diana rests. The moon, ascending,

makes a silver pathway through the forest,
shining on our merrymaking chorus
singing to the sister of Apollo,
"Everywhere Diana goes, we follow."

Echo
(A Nymph's Lament)

Her laughter filled this quiet wood–
Echo, my lost friend. We stood
in this clearing countless times
telling secrets, plotting childhood crimes.
Echo could talk; she was undone
by her own persuasive tongue,
which ran as swift as any deer.
She made gossiping a career
yet offended neither nymph nor sprite,
bringing everyone delight.
Her voice was pleasing, clear as a brook,
until Hera, in a blind rage, took
revenge on her for protecting me;
I was the guilty one, not she!
I was the one who danced and played
with Zeus in the forest's dappled shade,
while Echo endured the cruelest fate;
she sacrificed, for friendship's sake,
her greatest gift, her powers of speech.

Like water just beyond the reach
of a thirsty soul, her voice became
a torment–a curse. She lived in shame,
hiding behind rocks and trees
because of the many cruelties
inflicted by her so-called friends–
if only we could make amends,
but the time is past for apologies.
In truth, she made us ill at ease,
repeating everything we'd say.
I seldom think of her, but today
the smell of pine, wind in the trees,
stir this forest of memories
and shroud it in a mist of tears–
Echo, after all these years,
    I still–I regret–
        can't forget,
           can't forget.

Muses' Song IV
Hearth Chant

Hestia, draw near us—
keep alive the flame!
Gentle goddess, hear us;
Hestia, draw near us
with warmth and light to cheer us
as we gather in your name.
Hestia, draw near us—
keep alive the flame!

Remembrance
(Nymph's Song)

Watch him in his hiding place,
where woodland shadows fall like lace
at meadow's edge. The sun is bright;
he'll disappear in dappled light

until a momentary beam
causes moss green eyes to gleam,
revealing him. When you see him rise
on shaggy haunches to mountain-size,

hold your breath. He'll turn your way
with pipes in hand and begin to play
a forgotten tune sad Echo repeats
over faraway hills, where the day retreats.

Remember the sound—pure, bright.
Remember the way he springs from sight—
like a deer, yet a man—
on cloven hooves. Remember Pan.

Ganymede's Song

When night falls on Olympus,
the gods go home to bed.
I'll hear their footsteps echo
down the marble halls and dread

the silence that surrounds me
with the darkness. In my room,
I'll feel as if I'm trapped inside
a stone-cold tomb.

I'll lie awake and wonder
if the royal flocks of Troy
still nestle in the fragrant hills
I wandered as a boy.

I'll close my eyes and see myself
surrounded by my sheep
beside a blazing campfire,
drifting off to sleep.

When night falls on Olympus,
my spirit's free to roam
above the moonlit treetops
far away–home.

Appendix I: Mount Olympus

Ares (Roman, Mars): Arrogant, brutal son of Zeus and Hera and god of war who was hated by all on Mount Olympus—with the notable exception of Aphrodite, goddess of love, who (for reasons none of her fellow gods and goddesses understood) remained deeply in love with him in spite of her marriage to Hephaestus, god of the forge.

Athena (Roman, Minerva): Warrior goddess of wisdom and patroness of useful arts. She is said to have sprung from Zeus's head in full armor, clutching her invincible spear and uttering a fierce battle cry. She is also called Pallas Athene.

Ganymede: Young Trojan shepherd-prince who was carried off by Zeus (disguised as an eagle) to Mount Olympus. He became the gods' cupbearer and was given immortality.

Helios (Roman, Sol): God of the sun who drove a chariot with four horses across the heavens every day, from east to west. Because he saw everything that happened on Earth during his daily crossing, he was often portrayed in stories as a witness to human events. He is often confused with Apollo, the Olympian god of the sun, but Helios represents the sun in its daily course while Apollo represents the sun's illuminating power.

Hephaestus (Roman, Vulcan): God of the forge, son of Zeus and Hera, supreme craftsman who built the palaces on Mount Olympus and made the thunderbolts of Zeus. He was crippled by Zeus, who threw him out of heaven after an argument with Hera. Hephaestus fell for a full day before landing on the island of Lemnos. He was married to Aphrodite, the goddess of love.

Hera (Roman, Juno): Goddess of marriage, queen of Olympus, and jealous wife of Zeus. She is the mother of Ares, Hephaestus, Hebe, and Eris.

Mount Olympus: The highest mountain in Greece, it was the home of the twelve gods and goddesses known as the Olympians. They lived in an enormous palace at the top of the mountain, high above the clouds.

Muses: Nine sisters born of Zeus and Mnemosyne, the goddess of memory: Clio, Euterpe, Thalia, Melpomene, Terpsichore, Erato, Polyhymnia, Urania, and Calliope. They sang and danced at Olympian festivities and inspired mortals to create all forms of literary art. They were invoked especially by poets and musicians.

Zeus (Roman, Jupiter or Jove): Supreme ruler of the gods. The son of titans Cronos and Rhea, he overthrew his titan forbears and established a new order on Mount Olympus. He was the father of many Olympians, including twins Apollo and Artemis, Hephaestus, Ares, Hermes, and Persephone. He was both father and mother to Athena, who sprang full-grown from his head.

Appendix II: The Sea

Acetes: Kindly helmsman who tried to stop his crewmates from kidnapping Dionysus. He alone was spared when Dionysus punished his captors by changing them into dolphins.

Aphrodite (Roman, Venus): Greek goddess of love and beauty who was believed to have arisen from the sea. She floated to the island of Cyprus, where she was adorned by the Seasons and escorted to Mount Olympus. She was the mother of Eros (Roman, Cupid) and the wife of Hephaestus, but her true love was Ares, the god of war.

Dionysus (Roman, Bacchus): God of wine and fruitfulness, son of Zeus and the mortal Semele. The celebration of his rites was marked by the wild frenzy of his female devotees, called Maenads. Once kidnapped by a band of pirates who mistook him for a wealthy youth, Dionysus changed them into dolphins.

Naxos: Largest of a group of Greek islands known as the Cyclades. It was considered to be the home of Dionysus.

Poseidon (Roman, Neptune): God of the sea, son of titans Cronos and Rhea, and brother of Zeus and Hades. When the titans were overthrown, the three brothers cast lots for rulership of the world. Zeus received the sky, Poseidon the sea, and Hades the underworld.

Venus de Milo: Famous ancient Greek statue representing Aphrodite, created by an unknown sculptor around 1–30 B.C. It was named *Venus de Milo* because a peasant found it on the Greek island of Milos in 1820. It was broken in two and missing its arms. The statue was later repaired and given to King Louis XVIII of France. It is a popular tourist attraction at the Louvre museum in Paris, France, where it is now exhibited.

Appendix III: The Underworld

Cerberus: Three-headed dog that guarded the entrance to the underworld.

Charon: Surly old ferryman who took the spirits of the dead across the River Styx to Hades' realm. The trip wasn't free; Greeks traditionally placed a coin in mouths of deceased loved ones to pay Charon his fare.

Demeter (Roman, Ceres): Goddess of the harvest, of fruitfulness and vegetation. Like Zeus, she is the daughter of titans Cronos and Rhea. Her daughter, Persephone, was abducted by Hades and later became his wife. The earth was ravaged by drought and famine while Demeter grieved for her stolen daughter. The Olympians pleaded with her to accept the marriage and restore the dying world, but she steadfastly refused. Zeus sent Hermes to the underworld to convince Hades to send Persephone back to her mother. Hades agreed, but tricked the girl into eating seven pomegranate seeds. Because she had eaten the fruit of the dead, she was forced to return to the underworld. Zeus struck a bargain between Demeter and Hades that allowed Persephone to spend half the year with her mother. The other half Persephone spent in the underworld with Hades.

Fates: Three elderly sister-goddesses who were said to control the destinies of humans, presiding over every birth and death. Lachesis assigns each individual his or her fate, Clotho spins the individual's thread of life, and Atropos wields the dreaded scissors that cut the thread when a life is over.

Furies: Three snake-haired sisters, older than the Olympians, who punished the guilty by driving them mad with fear. They were named Alecto (the unresting), Megaera (the jealous), and Tisiphone (the avenger).

Hades (Roman, Pluto): God of the underworld, one of three sons of the titans Cronos and Rhea, brother of Zeus and Poseidon. After the titans were overthrown, the three brothers divided the conquered world between them. As ruler of the underworld he controlled the earth's buried wealth of gold, silver, and precious stones. Forbidden to visit Olympus, Hades grew lonely living among the dead. He contrived, with Zeus's consent, to make Persephone his unwilling bride.

Hermes (Roman, Mercury): Son of Zeus and Maia, he was known as the swift messenger-god who delivered Zeus's messages to intended recipients on Earth and was given the nightly task of escorting the dead to Hades. Hermes is also known as the god of good luck and wealth and patron of merchants and thieves. He was exceedingly clever and good-natured.

Morpheus: Son of Hypnos, the god of sleep. He was called the "bringer of dreams."

Nymphs: Spirits in the form of young maidens who inhabited woods, trees, and mountains. They often served as attendants to the goddesses.

Persephone (Roman, Proserpina): Queen of the underworld, unhappy wife of Hades. Her abduction by Hades caused dreadful conditions on the earth. Her yearly return from the world of the dead heralds spring.

Sirens: Half-women, half-birds who lured sailors to their death with enchanting songs. They were wood nymphs once, companions of Persephone and witnesses to her abduction. They searched everywhere for their lost friend, but never found her. The gods gave them wings to continue their quest over the sea.

Styx: Best known of the five rivers of hell, it wound five times around the underworld. The grim ferryman Charon carried the dead across it in his boat.

Appendix IV: The Forest

Apollo: Greek god of the sun, patron of art, music, and medicine. Son of Zeus and Leto, he is the twin brother of Artemis.

Artemis (Roman, Diana): Goddess of the hunt and protector of infants, both animal and human. She is the daughter of Zeus and Leto and twin sister of Apollo. Like her brother, Artemis is connected to the healing arts and imparted her knowledge of medicinal herbs and wildflowers to her followers. Her brother is known as Phoebus the sun god (Phoebus means "shining"); Artemis is associated with the moon. She is also a much older god than Apollo, and was worshiped in other cultures long before the Greeks installed her on Mount Olympus. Diana, her Roman counterpart, is also thought to be much older than the Olympians. They were arguably the most powerful, complex goddesses in the Greco-Roman pantheon.

Echo: Forest nymph who was known as a chatterbox. When Zeus was visiting with one of the nymphs in the forest, Echo engaged Hera in a long conversation that allowed Zeus and his friend time to escape. Hera discovered the trick and punished Echo by taking away her power of speech. Allowed only to repeat what others said, Echo's grief caused her to waste away until nothing was left but her answering voice.

Hestia (Roman, Vesta): Goddess of the hearth, of peace and family, honored eldest sister of Zeus. She sought solitude and anonymity and is the only Olympian for whom no physical representation was ever made. She was thought to be present in the hearth flame that was tended with great ceremony and reverence in every Greek home.

Pan (Roman, Sylvanus or Faunus): Country god of herds and flocks and ruler of the nature spirits. Pan had the body of a man, but the horns, ears, and legs of a goat. He frequented caves and lonely, rural places and played hauntingly beautiful melodies on the syrinx, a simple instrument he invented. Called "panpipes" in honor of the god, they are still played today.

Bibliography

Bell, Robert E. *Women of Classical Mythology.* New York: Oxford University Press, 1993.

Bulfinch, Thomas. *Myths of Greece and Rome.* Compiled by Bryan Holme with an introduction by Joseph Campbell. New York: Penguin Books, 1981.

Davenport, Guy, translator. *7 Greeks.* New York: New Directions Books, 1995.

Evans, Bergen. *Dictionary of Mythology, Mainly Classical.* New York: Dell, 1970.

Godolphin, R. B., ed. *Great Classical Myths.* New York: Random House, 1964.

Graves, Robert. *Greek Gods and Heroes.* New York: Dell, 1960.

Hesiod. *Theogony, Works and Days.* Translated by M. L. West. Cambridge: Oxford University Press, 1988.

Lucian. *Selected Satires of Lucian.* Edited and translated by Lionel Casson. New York: W. W. Norton & Co., 1968.

Ovid. *Metamorphoses.* Translated by Horace Gregory. New York: Mentor Books, 1960.

Sappho. *Sappho: A Garland.* Translated by Jim Powell. New York: Farrar, Straus, Giroux, 1993.